ALSO BY TIM LUCAS

FICTION
Throat Sprockets (1994)
The Book of Renfield: A Gospel of Dracula (2005)
The Only Criminal (forthcoming)
The Man With Kaleidoscope Eyes (forthcoming)

NON-FICTION
Your Movie Guide to Movie Classics Video Tapes and Discs
   (with Alex Gordon, 1985)
Your Movie Guide to Science Fiction Video Tapes and Discs
   (1985)
Your Movie Guide to Horror Video Tapes and Discs
   (1985)
*Your Movie Guide to Mystery/Suspense Video Tapes
   and Discs* (1985)
The Video Watchdog Book (1992)
Mario Bava: All the Colours of the Dark (2007)
Studies In The Horror Film: Videodrome (2008)
Midnight Movie Monographs: *Spirits of the Dead (Histoires
   Extraordinaires)* (2018)
Midnight Movie Monographs: *Succubus (Necronomicon)*
   (forthcoming)

The SECRET LIFE of LOVE SONGS

The SECRET LIFE of LOVE SONGS

TIM LUCAS

ISBNs

978-1-786367-02-0
978-1-786367-03-7 (signed edition)

Design & Layout by Michael Smith
Printed in England by T.J. Books

PS Publishing Ltd
Grosvenor House
1 New Road
Hornsea, HU18 1PG
England

editor@pspublishing.co.uk
www.pspublishing.co.uk

ACKNOWLEDGEMENTS

THIS NOVELLA WAS originally written between 2008 and 2012 for a projected anthology of fiction inspired by the music of Nick Cave that never materialized. Asked to pick something of his for the basis of my story, I chose his lecture *The Secret Life of the Love Song*, a spoken-word recording encompassing five songs which was issued on CD by King Mob in 2000.

Should any clarification be necessary, this is not that.

This is a work of fiction. Any resemblance of characters to actual persons, living or dead, is a blend of the tributary and the purely coincidental.

'A Broken Appointment' by Thomas Hardy quoted from *Collected Poetry* (London: MacMillan and Company, 1919).

Five of the songs included within this work—'Desert Mariner', 'Under the Nine', 'Ambidextrous Heart', 'The Smell of Cedar (A Walk Through the Woods)' and 'Trust In Love'—were originally written for this novella as poetry. They were later set to music by Dorothy Moskowitz and the author from 2017-2020. A sixth song, 'Broken' was also co-written by Dorothy and I, this time in adaptation of the aforementioned Thomas Hardy poem. All of our songs are published and copyrighted 2020 by Oh You Kid Publishing, BMI.

For all of the Ds
And also Nick, for their inspiration.

And in loving memory of
Robert Uth (195–2020)
Who led me to the novelist in myself.

PROLOGUE

THE HOUSE LIGHTS DIM, severing innumerous whispered conversations had amounted collectively to a low yet excited roar. Emerging from the wings at stage right is the Lecturer, his eagerly awaited entrance warmly received by his audience. As he hastens into public view, he clutches to his breast a manila folder containing the typewritten substance of this evening's talk. The first thing his audience notices about him, seen in person this way, is his peculiar way of walking. Bent over almost by half, with his forehead leading the way, he appears to be urged forward by the divining rod of his own stubborn will.

He nods a shy and mildly flustered acknowledgement of the warm reception as his inclining gait leads him to the illuminated lectern at centre stage. Once there, he taps the microphone, opens his manuscript, then does the improper thing in this temple of academia by lighting a Consolations cigarette. With this insolent gesture, the Lecturer owns the room.

Familiar from the covers of myriad recorded works, the Lecturer's face is pallid and angular, his brooding eyes a blue bright enough to be seen without binoculars from as many as twenty rows away, conveying the soul of a poet below a hawkish, hooded brow. His long hair, as black as his suit of clothes, is worn straight and swept back, overhanging his white collar like sharpened teeth. His outfit is not quite tailored to his frame and suggests the hand-me-down property of an evangelical father or perhaps an older brother in the funeral business. He has the cultivated look of a refugee from a lost manuscript of Flannery O'Connor, a harbinger unhinged by the calamitous force of his own prophecies.

When he finally speaks, it is with a stentorian solemnity that borders on the penitent.

Good evening, he begins, shielding his eyes with one hand while squinting past the stage lights for any glimpse of friendly faces that might be tucked deep into the attending shadows. As you know, the subject of my lecture tonight is the Love Song. Though the songs I've written and recorded over the past thirty years might easily be mistaken for something else, as the growing body of criticism about them tends to support, I have always considered the great bulk of them to be love songs. The stories they tell may be dark and weird, sometimes no one emerges from the lyric alive or even sane, but underlying all of them is a common germ I consider central to all my best writing: that galvanic moment when two strangers meet and are forever changed—or, to use the Biblical term, smited (or should that be 'smitten'?)—by the experience.

To paraphrase a well-worn but eternally apt lyric, the Love Song is a many splendoured thing. There are love songs that declare love, define, describe, declaim and even deny love. Others lament the loss of love, the bungling of love, the messy untimeliness of love.

The most popular ones tend to celebrate the miracle of reciprocated love, while a great many more wallow in the morass of unrequited affections, twisting the knives left to rot in hearts that might otherwise cease to feel anything more whatsoever. There are love songs for Muses, for valentines and mistresses, for mothers and fathers, for brothers and sisters; there are songs that soar with the love of God and fellow veterans. There is an interesting paucity of love songs addressed to husbands and wives.

All love songs have a purpose, but these purposes are not always the same. Some render honour, while others aspire to seduce. Some entice us to slip away, while others suggest we do it in the road. Some look away from the rhythmic animal rutting that those eighteen-minute Isaac Hayes tracks have been known to induce, compiling instead the sentimental lists of love's ephemera—the cigarettes that bear the lipstick traces, the airline tickets to romantic places. Some love songs strain all the cords in their necks to confirm for us, in our romantic desolation, that love still exists.

"There is no love in this world anymore," sings Pete Shelley of the Buzzcocks, knowing full well this can't be true in a world where such a despairing sentiment can still be sung with such feeling. The singer stands as proof of the contrary. Some love songs serve to sweeten the tears that contented love causes to well in our eyes, while others offer skeleton keys for those locks buried deep within us that hold back the most stubborn tears. There are love songs that aren't even love songs; that, when their first familiar notes are transmitted by our car radio, makes us roll down our window, no matter how cold the evening, and hang

5

our heads outside to brave the oncoming breeze as we undergo an abstract form of romance without goal, existing only to be lived through once again. We all have songs like that; you all know yours; for me, that song might be 'Telstar' or 'Sukiyaki' or even 'Cortez The Killer.'

Yes, the love song is a great many things to a great many people: a daydream, a lubricant, a lament, a confidant, a blueprint for action, a subpoena, a rabbi, an emetic, a dominant, a Will-o'-the-wisp, a bowl of chicken soup, a cock ring, a Kleenex, a translator of raw emotion into words that chime with truth and clarity in the mind—truth and clarity, so often uninvited guests in our affairs of the heart.

To write a love song today, in the twenty-first century, seems as quixotic a notion as taking two feral cats by the scruffs of their necks and forcing them to mate by hand, considering how many there already are in the world. Almost fifty years ago, Paul McCartney asked if we hadn't already had enough of the damned things, and proceeded to score another number one hit with his musical question. Nevertheless, they keep on coming, clarifying, redefining, performing public autopsies on the beating heart of love. To hear a love song, even the most cloying or tedious of them, as one's belly rests heavily on the barbed and honeyed wire of the emotion itself, is to feel less alone... in the stark and spacious nakedness of what we feel, more articulate and aware in the face of Love's devastating, godly immensity.

And now, my first example.

I

A SUDDEN SPHERE OF turquoise light near stage left, to the Lecturer's immediate right, slowly dilates to reveal a lonely-looking Yamaha KX88 Synthesizer keyboard. The Lecturer abandons his lectern for the instrument, absent-mindedly carrying his sheaf of papers with him as he takes a seat in front of the instrument. He places them beside him on the bench as the stage lights dim and prompt receptive applause, lending definition to a lambent, submarine atmosphere.

The Lecturer leans over the keys of the instrument, gazing down upon the staggered planks of white and black with an *appassionata* that might be caressing or murderous. The open microphone in front of him inadvertently picks up a few words he mutters to himself and perhaps intends no one else to hear, something that sounds like "Look at me..."

—and then, when the moment finally nods its assent, his large pale hands fall upon the keyboard with a neatly penetrating tenderness.

The sound of the instrument is cool, mellow, and mentholated. The opening notes induce an almost magical suspension of time. Before a word is sung, a melody—or at least a method— takes shape in the rippling recurrence of an introductory, incantatory figure, causing the assembled listeners to picture a body of tremulous water pierced here and there by soft shafts of forlorn light. Once this picture has been painted, there emerges from these prestidigitated fathoms the voice everyone in this auditorium has come to hear. It is a voice capable of summoning what one critic described as "a gospel growl"...however, in the setting of this particular number, it lets itself be heard in all its honest tenderness, striking the note of a lone but virile heart reaching out to an ever-receding, perhaps mythic shore.

DESERT MARINER

Till Friday she would be away
And he'd be on his own.
So, four days out of five that week,
The swimmer swam alone.
Her warning was a caring one,
Thought he—a drought foretold.
But midway through, the swimmer knew,
He could not be consoled.
He could not be consoled.

The swimmer flailed that Tuesday
Where once he used to glide,
Carving through the waves she made

As she swam close beside.
What kept him moving forward
Was trusting she'd return
Adrift but ever shoreward
He knew she would return.
Perhaps she would return.

Desert mariner, amid
The blue and glassy dunes,
Shouldering the shallows
As a Siren calls the tunes.

Their pool became a barren place
An Anvil of the Sun
The swimmer parched and lost
Without her laughter and her fun.
Bit by bit, his laps collapsed.
His pounding heart declared,
"If home is where the heart is,
Then I'm only halfway there.
I'm only halfway there."

She'd left him with a solemn vow
To his heart, he held it near.
When hope grew dim, words came to him
To help him persevere:
"If these four days have been a drought,
Then water she must be!
Tears, rebirth—an ocean's worth,
All surrounding me.
All surrounding me.

9

Desert mariner, amid
The blue and glassy dunes,
Shouldering the shallows
As a Siren calls the tunes.

The song somehow thrives in its murmuring and murmurs to a close, ending so quietly that it takes its listeners a few extra moments for their hands to find one another in acclamation. By the time silence returns to the room, the Lecturer has returned to the podium and a different, whiter funnel of light as the keyboard is swallowed once more in attending darkness.

THE SONG YOU'VE JUST heard, he announces, is entitled 'Desert Mariner'. It is a saga, an ancient legend, even a sob story, but it is first and foremost a love song, written as an expression of love that could be expressed in no other way, to a woman who was, and is, unavailable—as I am. 'Desert Mariner' is a snapshot of romantic love, impossible love, quixotic love. It keeps faith with the unsure, curbing it, willing it into certainty. It is an oath of patience and devotion that says "I will wait. I will wait for you—even if you never come." The swimmer is determined to reach his object of desire, with the will of someone who can turn a desert into an ocean. It's a solemn daydream of romance that could only have been written by someone who knows and values the concept of romantic fidelity. I wrote the song and, regardless of what you may think of me from what I've said so far, I am just such a person. My heart may strain against its leash at times, but it's loyal. Sometimes in more than one direction.

The audience, in different pockets, chuckles.

10

I married at a very young age, the Lecturer continues. Even so, my love for my Wife was and remains a mature love, a deep and abiding love consecrated, first and above all else, in friendship. I signed up for the long haul with no prior knowledge of women; I never got to experience an intimacy with the kind of woman who might have impressed me as being "my type." If you're familiar with my recorded work, you know the sort of women I sing about; they are ravenspawn, dark-haired and brooding, impish, intuitive, acerbic, nail-biting; they reside at the bottom of my shot glass with their chapped lips and bad habits and oracular gazes, glancing my way with expressions far stranger and more calculating than kindness.

I think of these creatures, their thumbs perpetually out on the open roads of my imagination, as my "sullen brunettes." After a lifetime of contemplating this species, all that I really know about them is that they do not love me—much as the original sullen brunette, my mother, did not love me. She ceased to love me after the death of my father, who was taken from her in an automobile accident when I was only nine years old. I resembled my father, and because my widowed mother could not bear to look at me, she turned me out and I went to live with my paternal grandparents in Maine, where I continued my schooling.

Knowing the psychological reason for their bat-like infestation of my creativity does nothing to inure me to the charms of my sullen brunettes. On every album I've ever made, sullen brunettes litter my lyric sheets like the stones on a pebble beach—and yet, in the smartest move I ever made, I took a California blonde as my Wife. She is my best friend and I love her without question or limit, but she has never figured in anything I've written or recorded—and don't think for one minute that she hasn't noticed.

11

The audience laughs, presenting the Lecturer with the opportunity to take another long draw on his cigarette, which he then drops to the floor of the stage, crushing it under the Cuban heel of a blue suede boot.

I won my Wife's heart, and she mine, through the discipline of correspondence. At the time of our first, accidental and very brief meeting, she had done me a great kindness, at a time in my life when kindness was rare. On impulse, as though prompted by a godly whisper in my ear, I reached out to her with pen and paper—without remembering what she looked like. She wrote back to me and we continued writing.

We were both journal keepers and our journal entries gradually curtailed as we began to address our innermost thoughts and daily adventures to one another. By the time we met for the second time, after a month of almost daily missives, we were already deeply attached. The fact that she was a blonde with Renaissance features and didn't look anything like other girls I might have pursued didn't matter. At a young and tender age, I somehow found the wisdom to love her soul more than her image as much as her flesh, ever so slightly more orange than my own paler hue. Over the years, my love of her has had the effect of amplifying her physical characteristics into one of my abiding standards of female beauty. This is not to say I'm now attracted to every California blonde that I see, because my Wife is all California blondes to me; what I mean to say is that, because of her and the standard she established in my experience, I am now able to appreciate the beauty in other women cast in her image.

My Wife is my bedrock, my centre of gravity, my sanity, and perhaps for that reason, as I say, she and my creativity have never coincided. Consequently, my art has always been akin to an unrepentant adulterer, ever dependent on those sullen brunettes I have known and taken to heart—always from afar.

'DESERT MARINER' WAS written a year or so ago in late summer, as I was coming out of one of the most difficult periods in my life. It's hard to explain why it was difficult. It should have been a time of great fulfillment and joy, but it wasn't. Let me try to explain... A couple of years ago, I released an album called *The Atlas of What Lives and Breathes*...

The audience responds to its mention with warm enthusiasm.

My album before that had been quite successful, successful enough to buy me some time, which I lavished unwisely (but, I felt, necessarily) on its successor. *The Atlas of What Lives and Breathes* became my first new recorded work in ten years, a project so long in gestation that my preoccupation with it changed the way I looked at and thought of myself. While in the depths of it, I felt so convinced of its importance that I was afraid it might be all that I need ever achieve, and that its end would commence the countdown to my mortality. In other words, I reached a point where I believed that, as long as I kept writing and fine-tuning the songs for this collection, I might live forever.

I was finally able to cut my cord with the album. It was very well received and sold extremely well, but none of this made any difference to me. It was while I was on the road promoting it that I began to feel the terrible void left in me by its completion. Sometimes in concert I found myself tinkering with songs I couldn't possibly improve, as a means of trying to reintroduce myself into their space. When the tour finally ended, when I was no longer living those songs on a nightly basis, I began to feel not just empty but abandoned. I felt *bereft*.

13

My Wife, seeing how unhappy I was, suggested, as I didn't have a project currently at hand, that I make a project of myself. I knew what she meant: my involvement with my *Atlas* had turned me into someone far more sedentary and cerebral, moreso than the man she had married, and as you might imagine, my being on the road had rekindled some old self-destructive habits. Bolivian marching powder, jazz cigarettes, and that kind of thing. I was in no better condition physically than I was mentally, but I had never been able to apply myself for very long to the tedium of walking and weight training. The only form of exercise I ever enjoyed was swimming, so she encouraged me to seek out a nearby health facility with an indoor pool—someplace where I could swim whenever I wished, regardless of weather or season.

I found a local hospital facility that accepted memberships of all ages while specializing in fitness training for retirees. The place itself was a bit long in the tooth, with hot tubs that were always breaking down and rusty patches on the cream-coloured piping above the pool that I studied while floating along on my back. It was staffed by the kind of women you see at bake sales. It was not a sexy place.

I began swimming three times a week in their five hundred-meter pool that winter. To be honest, I had not been in an ocean or a pool since the turn of the century, and it was a struggle at first to regain my muscle memory and the synchronicity of my upper and lower limbs under the half-amused gaze of the hung-over kids employed by the place as lifeguards. By my third visit, I could feel my former capability, my posture, my stamina returning.

I went as early in the morning as I could bear, because I preferred to swim when the pool was all mine. The stiller and less competitive the waters, the more calmly and sensually I could

14

take my exercise, without my neighbouring swimmers turning each lap into a race. The water in the pool gradually became a sensitive extension of my own skin. I would swim to exhaustion and catch my breath while squatting in the shallow end; there, I became absorbed in the sight of the overhead piping reflected on the page of blue water my actions had left tremulous, the settling waves sending peristaltic spasms through them until they were fully becalmed, my signal to push off once again. There was an inevitable sense of intrusion when some obese or otherwise hobbled male or female took their tentative steps down the four stone steps into the shallow end, intruding into my fantasy of timeless solitude. They were annoyances, but not nearly so upsetting as having the peace of the place obliterated by those barrel-chested men who plunged into the depths like cannonballs and punched their passages across the pool's exploding surface; I always saw their blunt swimming as advertisements for the appalling, thrashing ways they made love.

When one of these fellows became a standard feature of my 11:00 a.m. visits, I rethought my schedule and began arriving at the pool closer to noon. For some reason, probably the lunch hour, it was harder to claim an open lane at noon, but the pool was almost always mine alone as the hour edged closer to one. I started sleeping in an hour later. After 1:00 p.m., I almost always had the pool to myself for at least the first twenty minutes of my workout. I kept my focus on the sandals I left on the ledge at the deep end, where it was my habit to plunge in, or on the clock mounted on the wall at the shallow end, taking little or no notice of other swimmers who came along as I began to tire.

A couple of weeks into this routine, a fellow swimmer suddenly took the lane next to mine, whose presence I could feel *literally dyeing* the water with electric sexual tension.

15

Looking over my right shoulder with every other stroke as I free-styled past her, I would catch little glimpses: a surfacing breast, almost flattened and tightly sheathed in navy blue, as she swam on her back; the blur of a butterfly tattoo; a languid but toned bare leg kicking past; a peach-like behind briefly breaking the surface in the execution of a perfect tuck-and-roll.

Once or twice, we found ourselves standing side by side in the shallows, catching our breaths, but we didn't speak or look directly at one another. She wore blue goggles and a bathing cap that matched her suit. When I sneaked looks at her through my mirrored goggles, I could read nothing in her face except a focused determination to swim another lap, another, then another.

She wasn't there every day, and I began to notice when she wasn't. Then there came a day when we both traversed the pool together in perfect harmony, stroke for stroke...That's when I knewin the pit of my stomach that words were going to be spoken at some point, possibly decisive ones. I swam another lap while mulling this over and, by the time I returned to the shallows, her lane was empty, wet footprints leaving a rapidly evaporating trail to the ladies' shower room.

One afternoon, I had the place again entirely to myself—the lifeguard, a tall blonde with no hips and long straight legs, had retreated into her little office to text a friend. I swim by the clock and don't count my laps, but I imagine I had done close to forty when I swam toward the shallow end with the idea of calling it a day. Swimming blind, I tagged the pool wall and clung to it, eyes closed, my breathing hammer-hard as my legs sailed behind me like limp flags in the rippling water. When I opened my eyes, there she was—sitting next to me on the ledge of the pool, her calves submerged and zigzagging in the crystal blue water.

16

"You're in a whole different league today," she said, chuckling at the state I was in.

As I struggled to recollect myself, she asked how many laps I had done. As I said, I hadn't been counting but I coughed out a best estimate, which made her laugh. I must have sounded like I'd just fucked half the Rockettes.

The audience laughs, giving the Lecturer time to wet his whistle with a tumbler of water left thoughtfully at the podium.

She was my junior by at least a decade and cursed merrily, like a sailor. I was old enough to remember when the use of such words carried significant consequences, but she had never known a time when they were not her birthright. I wasn't offended by her cursing—my own songs are rife with it; if anything, I took her openness as a compliment—she was a person of a certain generation, speaking to me as a peer in tribal candor, in an environment where people in our general age group were scarce. She may have deployed her carnal epithets, in the funny way she did, for the same reason she spoke to me in the first place: to discharge a sexual tension she had also felt permeating the waters we shared.

There was a moment during our first conversation when I stepped back in my mind from what was happening and could not remember a time when we weren't talking, when she wasn't by my side—comic, anatomic, squalid, sublime. She was from Nantucket, I learned as Calliope, goddess of poetry, smiled, and when I stole a look at her hands I spied a wedding band. She had an apple-shaped face, an upturned nose I thought of as Dutch, and understated good looks she could bring to a flare with emphases from her pale blue eyes—all this was very unusual yet familiar to me. I've never had a taste for ostentatious beauty; I prefer a face that takes time to know properly, and hers was a

17

face that refused to be known at a glance. I kept looking, looking away and looking back, sometimes glimpsing the face of the mischievous child she had been, or the face of the sage and feisty, weathered old bird she was going to be. There was a feral quality about her, bound to her sense of fun, yet she was also possessed of a natural, yet classical, poise. Her hands and arms were well toned and expressive; when she gesticulated—she liked to talk with her hands—it was with a physical grace that I could imagine stringing celestial bows or rearranging constellations in the heavens. You know how men are.

As we compared notes on the pool, which we liked, and in more muttered tones bemoaned the otherwise decrepit state of the facility, I continued my inventory of her outer being in what quickly amounted to lyrical detail. I took eager note of her copper hair, her widow's peak, the Connecticut accent she used to speak, the blue gum in her mouth and her cream-coloured teeth, the navy blue Lycra she wore like a sheath, her auburn brows, her white-capped nails, her bare throat and all it entails...the flow of lyricism she released within me was immediate, as if sung from the beaks of the doves tattooed in a delicate spiral winding in ascent around the length of her left forearm.

She eased herself off the ledge and lowered her yoga-lithe body into the hip-deep water, where the blue and white banners hanging overhead were reflected in configurations like the suits of harlequins and playing cards. I was exhausted, on the point of climbing out, but her playful, enticing energy inspired me—indeed, *invited* me—to continue, to reach for a new plateau in my workout. I didn't wish to compete with her; I waited for her to swim to the other side, or halfway across, before setting out on my own again. I surprised myself by staying in the water another thirty or forty minutes, somehow invigorated by her mere proximity, which sent warmish currents my way whenever her smooth bare limbs scissored past mine.

I was about to stop and exclaim my own surprise when I looked over into her lane and saw that—in the midst of my slow and easy strokes—she had gone, without so much as a farewell.

I missed my chance to see her in the lobby as I was signing out, or in the parking lot, where I had hoped to find her in her street clothes and see what her hair was like, how far down it fell without her bathing cap—but, that very night, I began to write again, quickly producing the first song of any quality I had written since *The Atlas of What Lives and Breathes*.

I had found a new Muse.

II

THE SONG I WROTE that night was not 'Desert Mariner'—I'll be coming back to that —and it is not a song of enough relevance to be performed here this evening.

Groans from the gallery.

The point is, her arrival marked the end of my creative drought. Of course, in such random yet significant relationships, everything about our subsequent meetings came with a hint of surprise. Her subsequent visits to the pool coincided with mine too neatly to be accidental, especially as I remembered mentioning to her the details of my routine. The place was almost always ours alone. Our conversations always picked up exactly where they left off before—during periods of rest in the shallows or while we soothed our muscles in the sluggish jets of the hot tub, prior to a second round of laps—with no sense of time passing between them.

She sometimes made casual reference to a husband, a carpenter who spent most of his free time in their two-car garage tinkering with Harley-Davidsons. She described a man I couldn't help but like rather than resent and whenever she sketched his portrait in anecdotes, I felt something formerly proprietary in the connection I felt with her begin to *relax*—a sense that it was okay; I didn't have to fret about her; she was loved and appreciated and being well cared-for. Whatever it was, whatever was happening between us wasn't about that.

Few subjects between the two of us were off-limits. She was only coy in her preference not to introduce names into our relationship—perhaps I wasn't the first man she had spoken to in the pool. That said, through attentive listening, I found her to be as familiar with the shops and streets on the west side of town as I was with those on the east side, where I lived, and for this reason, needing to think of her with some kind of name, I began to think of this new and special friend as the Westside Girl.

To my relief, she didn't recognize me or know my music. Don't get me wrong—I'm glad that *you* know who I am, but knowing can lead to preconceived notions and her obliviousness to my work suited me fine. I did tell her I wrote songs, as lots of people do, and when I later confessed to this, she seemed both amused and flattered that she helped inspire one or two. Mind you, she never asked to *hear* them, but she was pleased when I referred to her as my Muse. She joked about it, asking me if this particular job happened to come with any health benefits.

"Only immortality in song," I smiled—and so did she.

We began meeting at the pool on a hopscotch schedule of Tuesdays, Thursdays and Sundays. As these every-other-afternoons flowed into weeks, she told me more about herself. She also told me things about myself that made me feel better known by her, maybe, than by anyone else. Without specifically alluding to *The Atlas of What Lives and Breathes*, I mentioned

21

having come through a long creative process that left me feeling depleted. She asked me if I knew anything about numerology.

"Not really," I admitted. "It that one of your hobbies?"

"Not a hobby. More of a practice."

She then asked me for the year, date and hour of my birth, did some quick mental math, and proceeded to make perfect and orderly sense of what had always seemed to me a disordered life. She told me that, regardless of whether or not I felt myself to be flailing, I was actually "right on track." She explained that my project had been completed during what had been, for me, a Seven year (a time of social withdrawal and creative focus); that the year I knew to be the time of my tour had been my Eight year (a time of attainment and recognition).

"And now," she told me, hesitating briefly on the threshold of the phrase, "you're...under the Nine."

A few scattered groups of hands in the audience applaud in elite recognition. The Lecturer looks up briefly in appreciation of this, but keeps his smile down and soldiers on.

I asked what this meant.

"Under the Nine," she told me, "you see the fruits of your labours. Under the Nine, you begin to take personal inventory; you scrutinize your old ideas, clear out all the old dead shit in your life—the interests that no longer interest you, everything that no longer serves you, the people who no longer love you, the people you no longer love. You feel the need to abandon your usual caution, to make some mistakes. You feel an irresistible itch to fuck with things. You eliminate outmoded patterns of behavior; sometimes it hurts like hell, but it's necessary to the attainment of your fullest human potential. You start making major changes in your approach to living, like getting off your ass and coming to this shithole to swim three times a week. You

22

start reaching out, talking to strangers, even n'er-do-wells like me. You experience dramatic changes in personal attitude and temper. Your escapist desires become more pronounced, harder to deny."

I jumped in. So, being under the Nine would mean I was becoming more sociable, hungrier for life, more in need of...?

I fell silent in my search for the right word.

She had it on the tip of her tongue: "Intercourse."

Showman that he is, the Lecturer pauses, allowing the loaded word to hang in the air over the heads of his audience like a dirty dirigible. They respond obligingly with some muted giggles.

He takes another sip from his glass, to water himself and milk the moment, then goes on.

I asked, then, if the Nine year was analogous to the Death card in the Tarot deck, knowing that this represented not literal death but transformation and the end of old ways. She surprised me by saying that it didn't, that the Nine year was actually related to a different Tarot card, the Five of Cups: "The Lord of Loss in Pleasure."

As the Westside Girl spoke, I found myself searching her cyanotic eyes, intuiting that I could see through them into the huddled faces of her ancestry, Dutch and Irish faces, all gathered together in the dark of her pupils like herds of immigrants; the men mostly farmers, miners, and sea-farers, their women all Muses and Medusas. Their combined mass seemed to be collectively vying to get some urgent message across to me, through her—I repeat—*cyanotic* eyes, possibly without her awareness; something perhaps to vouchsafe their survival into the next generation and beyond. At least this is what deep, delusional fools like me tell themselves when their blood rises, ringing and chiming in their ears with primal imperative.

I asked what came after a Nine year. A Ten year?

"A One year," she told me.

"And what comes along in a One year?" I inquired.

"New life," she told me. "The One year is related to the Six of Cups, 'The Lord of Pleasure.' Pleasure may be lost, but it always returns. There is always renewal so long as life continues. The card shows the influence of Six (Beauty) in the suit of Water (Emotions). The cups you see on the card are ready to be filled, poised...erect."

The moment between us was thickening my blood with desire, the desire one feels for someone wiser and more beautiful, and as I foolishly sat there in the water, trying to imagine what was at work between us, she discharged the energy by laughing and splashing me—beauty in a suit of water, incarnate.

All the sullen brunettes within me died screaming.

THE LECTURER LOOKS UP brightly and says, Such feelings must be met with force and in my line of work, force requires collaboration. If you know me, you probably know some of these people...

He upholds his right hand and the pleated curtains at the back of the stage suddenly part to reveal—to the surprise of one and all—the Lecturer's usual musical collaborators, men and women, arranged in a semi-circle of drums and wires, strung instruments and humming amplifiers. The spotlight, now yellow, rises once again on the Yamaha synthesizer that, now evident, holds pride of place within the arrangement of these other instruments. Once again, the Lecturer assumes his place at his keyboard. The female drummer's count-off synchronized everyone to a collective summoning of 4/4 elegance.

UNDER THE NINE

Where's my trip to Mars in a Lotus car?
Where's my Samba Club? Where's my Telstar?
Where's my catamaran to the Isle of Capri?
Where's that Summer of Love I never got to see?

Where's my flying reindeer?
And if that's not clear
Why have I remained here? Why have I remained here?
Under the Nine (repeat 3x)

Sometimes it takes someone who's outside your square
To come along and show you what is where
A different clue in their eyes, a different hue in their hair
You can even see a different you in their stare

The what and whys are unclear
But they won't disappear
Maybe I can stay here, maybe I can play here
Under the Nine (repeat 3x)

You may set your eyes on a shining star
But it orbits you from a place so far
It has no place for you, except where you are
So you stay where you are
And learn to love the scar.

You know your old life is gone
Things have all gone wrong
'Cause you've found a new angle

Your life up to now's been a hexagon
Now your square's a triangle
You're all in a tangle

Going too fast to steer
So you stumble and veer
Now there's no doubt there
I know that you're out there
Under the Nine (repeat 3x)

All I have is the memory
Of what you once gave me
All I have is the memory
Of what you once gave me
And it's not gonna save me.

All I have is the memory
Of what you once gave me
All I have is the memory
Of what you once gave me
And it's not gonna save me.

The band rocks on for another minute or two, until the threads of the violinist's bow hang in shreds of Angel's hair, but they leave no final ribbon on the package. Divining the correct moment in the fracas, the Lecturer thrusts an arm up high, his bony wrist shooting out several inches from his black sleeve, then lets it drop; at this signal, the band stops playing—so curtly, so perfectly timed to the full blackout of the house lights as to suggest a power failure.

Shocked silence erupts with an outburst of applause as the

Lecturer, who remains seated, fishes another cigarette from his breast pocket, which he fires up with a steel lighter flashed like a switchblade.

He now addresses the audience from his piano bench, yanking his vocal mic into service. The stage lighting narrows and blanches to a more neutral white as his fellow musicians—all but one—drop their instruments and file offstage.

Some of you may recognize that song as "Under the Nine." (Those who do take this moment to let the Lecturer know it.) In its dervish swirl of urgency, some might take one good look at me and describe "Under the Nine" as the *cri de coeur* of a mid-life crisis, but I believe the panic it describes to be consistent with the onset of new love in most, if not all, relationships. It is intended as a love song and it's called "Under the Nine" because at those times when we look into new eyes and feel something new coming back, we all stand on the same threshold. It's called "Do we or don't we?"

I suppose I could have given the song a more commercial title—like "Out There," which certainly would have fit—but the sentiments it expressed were so direct, so impossible to fictionalize, that it made me fearful—both as an artist and as a man. I felt that I had to release the song, in order—to invite into my life whatever mysterious changes the song was bidding, but, in my heart of hearts, I didn't want anyone to hear it—except maybe the Muse who had transmitted the edit that it be written. People tell me it could have been a hit but I deliberately buried it—as some of you seem to know—as the B-side of a single released last fall in just a few overseas territories.

He takes this moment to resume his place at the lectern.

In this song, I think you can hear that, whenever the Westside Girl and I swam together, I was oblivious to anyone else who

27

might have been in the pool, or in the world. When we talked, I felt simultaneously aroused to life and at peace with the world, as though her presence offered me an opportunity to evolve—as a human being, as a man, as a songwriter and musician—in ways I could no longer expect of my marriage, happy as it was. Because with happiness comes contentment, and art, though it needs an anchor to secure it, also demands a measure of restlessness, recklessness; it demands we feel alive, vulnerable, susceptible—even unsafe.

There is no doubt that, on some level, I wanted whatever was happening between us to become sexual, but this was not ordinary, thoughtless lust. All my former sexual fantasies had been abruptly retired, replaced by the single playful fantasy of grabbing the ankle of the Westside Girl as she swam past.

She made my heart pound with such vigor that blood was not only brought back into tight places, but rare birds were freed from lost glades; she was performing both cardiologic and psychic bypasses. Once I caught her staring candidly at my chest and, noticing that I'd taken notice, she told me that she could see my heart pounding. I tried blaming the fact of all the laps I'd just swum, and she nodded, knowing better. It hadn't entirely been a lie; it was true that regular cardiovascular exercise was something fairly new to me and, with each passing week, I could feel myself firming up, becoming a more physical, alert and—yes—sexual being.

In absence of answers come the questions. Was I falling in love with her? Had I already fallen? What does it mean to be "in love"? This is a question that has baffled scientists, theologians, philosophers, songwriters…not to mention adult filmmakers throughout the ages.

Regardless of accepted definitions, I believe that love must be genuinely reciprocated before we can truly be "in love". After all, nothing is ever real until at least two people agree upon it. And that's when you're in it, *mon pauvre salaud*; otherwise, the emotion, however sincerely felt, is indivisible from delusion. As for myself, I could admit to myself an infatuation, a romantic attachment for the Westside Girl, but I refused—I consciously *refused*—to consider that I might actually be in love with her.

At night, however, from the moment my head hit the pillow, my brain became a Roman candle, my restless thoughts sending brushfire through entire forests of erotic possibility. I would lie there, unable to sleep as I fantasized how the Westside Girl might look in her street clothes; I would insert us into numerous situations, from the casual to the urgent: I would imagine us crashing our shopping carts and looking at one another in surprise as we turned a corner in a neighborhood grocery store...chance encounters in libraries and airports...a hot rendezvous on a hotel stairwell...seeking her out as loud skies flashed red and black at the height of wartime, and taking advantage of the fall of civilization, the backdrop of looting, violence, death and destruction, to finally press my mouth to hers with all the ardour of a man in love.

When I did manage to sleep and dream, I could never recall the Westside Girl figuring in any of my actual dreams, but she was always the first and last thought in my waking mind. Other dreams I could readily recall, always involving other people I know or have known, but none concerned her. Yet there seemed to be nothing in my conscious thoughts that did not concern her, not a square inch on the map of my skin that did not pine for the playful clawing of her nails from the moment I was recalled to life.

There were times during the course of any given day or night when I had to get up from where I was sitting and walk to the farthest corners of the house, away from my Wife, just to speak her name aloud in the silence of my home—to prove to myself that there really was a link between the fantasy world in which I was living and the one in which the Westside Girl existed in three dimensions, miles away—somewhere on the other side of town.

There were times when she occasionally missed a day or two of swimming. On those days I did not see the Westside Girl, I felt the sort of emotion that tightens our vocal cords almost to the breaking point, though one has made no sound. The only viable means I found of combating that feeling was to sit at my computer's piano keyboard, forging new melodies, binding words and rhymes to them, all summoned to mind by thoughts of who and where and even what she might be.

There were times when my Wife poked her head into my studio to tell me she liked what she was hearing.

III

THE WESTSIDE GIRL'S advent into my life made clear that a new chapter of my existence had begun, a chapter wherein my fantasies would demand their right to become tangible and real. I found this prospect both thrilling and frightening—frightening because I can think of nothing more terrifying than finding myself separated or, worse still, alienated from my Wife, and the revolution of my emotions was forcing me to, at least theoretically, allow for this possibility.

Then—so coincidentally with these fretful thoughts of mine as to suggest she might be going through them as well—the Westside Girl stopped coming to the pool altogether on our designated days.

I couldn't imagine she had given up swimming altogether, so I tried shuffling the days and hours when I swam, hoping to find her taking advantage of a more convenient slot, a slot that might also work for me, but she was nowhere to be found. My preoccupation with her whereabouts began to interfere with my exercise. Sometimes I would get into my lane at the pool and just crouch in the water up to my neck, eyes trained on its surface trembling. I began paying special attention to local evening news reports about road accidents and obituaries of women taken too soon.

Eventually, I worked up the courage to inquire about her at the club's front desk, but it quickly became obvious—embarrassingly so—that I had no right to such information. After all, I didn't know her name and had only the vaguest physical description to offer, once it had been muted and distorted in a vain effort to keep my interest casual and innocent. I was becoming angry and embittered, as I continued to swim three times a week through waters dense with memories abruptly cut short. I sought the taste of her in the chlorine.

The Lecturer takes a sip of water.

Six weeks passed. As I recall, it was a Thursday. I had swum my laps and was on the point of climbing out and hitting the showers when, suddenly... there she was.

It took a few moments for me to accept that I was looking at her. The Westside Girl walked toward me in hip-deep water, extending her hand. There was nothing of her former ribald humor about her—she knew that she had disappointed me—but once I took her hand in mine, where it lingered for some heartbeats after I had relaxed my grip, she understood she had been forgiven. She took me into her confidence, but only so far, explaining that she had fallen victim to certain demons and keeping busy was her only means of keeping them at bay.

One of the things I had learned about the Westside Girl, through our past conversations, was that she was proud of having never surrendered a friendship; she was still in touch with friends from college, past employers, past lovers, even someone she had known in kindergarten. Whenever she mentioned these people unknown to me, how I envied them their more comprehensive knowledge of her life story, a story that I would, in all likelihood, never know. It had always been part of her generous and social nature to make herself available to friends, even to the friends of friends; it was a burden of character I knew well, because it is also one of the more admirable—and frankly irritating—traits of my Wife. She understood that she ran the risk of giving people too little of herself, by striving to be there for so many, but she could turn no one away whose need of her she sensed—not even me.

The more she told me about all the people she knew, all the extra work she was taking on, the more aware I became that she and I were unlikely ever to converge in the way I had hoped and so often imagined. It was in these zones of sorrow that I became most aware of how much she and my Wife were alike.

As I crouched in the water beside her, hands tucked into my armpits, listening, I felt blindsided by the thought that I would never have her, would neverhave her, would never know her kiss.

She explained that her new schedule would make it difficult for her to swim on weekdays, and weekends would be impossible. As she said this, I understood that she had come to the health club, suited up and climbed into the water not to swim, but to bring me this news. At least I was that important to her; it was a morsel. Mine to chew.

It goes without saying, I had absolutely no claim upon her, but the fact that she was standing there before me, hip-deep in harlequin waters where she didn't have time to be, explaining her new schedule, gave me some hint of a right, some hint of a claim

33

on her heart. This encouraged me to suggest that we could meet there at any time that might be convenient for her, even at short notice. She looked flustered as she told me that Saturdays and Sundays were absolutely out, because those were the days she gave 'him' (meaning her husband), but Thursday... Thursday might be a possibility—not regularly, not enough for anyone to notice, maybe just once in awhile... maybe just once.

I bit the bullet by requesting... no, *demanding* more than a maybe; I claimed my right to a *promise*.

The Westside Girl wasn't able to conceal a look of uncertainty but, as pressure gave way to pleading, she gave me her word. Then we began to swim, tentatively—as people will when they first dip into the waters of a contract. After swimming a few laps with me, more in leisure than urgency, she left the pool as if fleeing her promise in shame and leaving me by no means confident that she would honour her vow. When I found her gone, I stood in waters up to my neck, still rocking with the recent memory of our mirrored movements, feeling a chest-full of confusion. I got out, showered and dressed in record time, in the hopes of catching, or at least seeing her in the parking lot, with the copper crinkles of her long hair dry and hanging down, her makeup gone, dressed in her street clothes—but she was already gone.

One night during this period, I remember sitting in my study in search of distraction. I opened an anthology of British poetry and happened upon a Thomas Hardy poem entitled 'A Broken Appointment.' It had been written more than a century ago, long before the men of my generation sprouted hair, but his pained words located and painted me in my moment with surgical precision. Hearts have always beaten and broken the same as they do again and again with each new crop of *homo sapiens*, just as the same moon has always hung in the sky. Hardy is best-remembered as a novelist but his poetry offers solemn evidence of a man who explored and experienced a good many things on the cutting edge of love and loss.

These were his words:

> *You did not come,*
> *And marching Time drew on, and wore me numb*
> *Yet less for loss of your dear presence there*
> *Than that I thus found lacking in your make*
> *That high compassion which can overbear*
> *Reluctance for pure loving-kindness' sake*
> *Grieved I, when, as the hope-hour stroked its sum,*
> *You did not come.*
>
> *You love not me,*
> *And love alone can lend you loyalty;*
> *I know and knew it. But, unto the store*
> *Of human deeds divine in all but name,*
> *Was it not worth a little hour or more*
> *To add yet this: Once you, a woman, came*
> *To soothe a time-torn man; even though it be*
> *You love not me?*

The agonized words hang over the audience like something waiting to drop. The Lecturer steadies himself, gripping the sides of his lectern, and presses on.

Not every love song is based on direct experience; a love song can sometimes be passed like a baton or a torch from one poet's words to another, or indeed from one plane of a miserable sad sack's consciousness to another. There was something in Hardy's shattered incrimination, in our shared misadventures of the heart, that I felt empowered by and yes, which entitled me to transmute them into song.

This is how 'Broken' came about.

The Lecturer returns to his synth keyboard accompanied by anticipatory applause, looking perhaps a bit more drained by his candor than he expected to be. He settles onto the bench and then, after making a few adjustments to change the sound these keys will next produce, awaits the moment's long velvet cape to enfold and involve him. Once he feels that measure of solace and safety ensured, he finds the courage to sing—over a stately, bittersweet melody that could easily have belonged to another time as well as this.

BROKEN

You did not come
And as Time marched on to bitter truth
I did succumb.

Two turned to three
The hour fled and my heart
Bled and wept in misery.

Not just for the lack of your being there
But for finding a lack in your make
Of some compassion to override reluctance
For pure, loving kindness' sake.

At this interval, a blue funnel of stage lighting is directed toward the rear of the stage, where a lingering member of the

36

band—a young female multi-instrumentalist with long golden hair—raises a cherry-red flute to her lips, lending a further shade of sorrow to the confession.

You loved not me
And love alone could lend you loyalty.
I knew it then, I know it now,
And I will know it, I suppose, till the end of me.

Was it not worth a minute of your day
To come to me in grace
To listen and to dry my face,
Even though it be,
As any fool could plainly see,
You love not me?

Even though it be,
As any fool but I could see,
You love not me.

You loved not me.

Head down, the Lecturer hovers over his keyboard until once again the spell of performance is broken by audience approbation, at which point the slender blonde accompanist sprints backstage and the stage lighting once again is reset for the solo performer.

The Lecturer continues: I swam again the next Sunday and felt every leaden tick of the clock during the ninety minutes I had set aside for physical exercise. But on Tuesday—equidistant between Sunday and Thursday, High Noon (as I sing) on the Anvil of the

Sun—I tore across our pool because, that Tuesday, I both *loved* the water and *hated* the water.

TO RETURN TO THE STORY I set out to tell, it was on that agreed-upon Tuesday I swam alone that I wrote 'Desert Mariner'.

The words just came to me, blue and glassy dunes and all, as if from a million miles and years ago. The efforts of the swimmer in my song are timeless through no achievement of my own; they are the efforts of all men who love someone who is beyond them, and such efforts to exceed ourselves are eternal. I felt healed by its creation and profoundly, if perversely, grateful to my Muse for the uncertainty and pain that brought it into my range. It was not until I had written this song that I understood that *The Atlas of What Lives and Breathes* had been, at best, a milestone in my career—not a headstone.

Having written this song for the Westside Girl, it was deeply gratifying to me when, on the Thursday after the inconsolable Tuesday described in the lyric, she did indeed keep her vow by reappearing at the pool—not in the swimming lane next to mine, but in my lane, alerting me to her presence by playfully reaching out and grabbing my ankle.

A sly, humorous murmur ripples through the crowd.

When I finished writing the song, I had made a secret pack with myself—that, if the Westside Girl kept her appointment with me on Thursday, I would share the song with her... but, as it transpired, I did not. Unless she's sitting among you in this theater tonight, she has probably never heard it.

It took my own involuntary trepidation about this to show me how deeply committed I am to my Wife, to our marriage, and

38

that I had no real intention of staking any tangible claim on the romantic fantasy proposed by the Westside Girl. Despite my heightened emotions, I remained adamant in my knowledge that, whatever relationship this stranger and I had or would have together, it was not about stealing away and starting anew. It was about something else, something I had yet to determine or understand.

IV

IN RETROSPECT, THE Westside Girl proved a blessing to my marriage, which experienced a remarkable erotic renaissance, especially on those checkerboard days when we laughed and swam together. I never superimposed her face on my Wife in the times we made love; on the contrary, the excitement unleashed in my blood dissolved our decades-long familiarity and allowed me to see my Wife again as she looked to me when we were both young and in love for the first time.

My Wife has never been particularly tidy; I've picked her blue jeans off of the bedroom floor countless times, but during this period, I found myself handling them with greater awareness and care. As I held them to eye level to fold them, I would press them to my chest and ask myself how the hips and thighs that formed my entire universe could possibly inhabit an article of clothing so small, how apparel so plain could inherit such dimensions of beauty simply by being worn.

After years of familiarity breaking down into routine, and routine breaking down into occasional dysfunction, our lovemaking now gained in frequency and spontaneity, feeling and intensity, just as all the varied aspects of my life and creativity were then gaining speed from the quickening of my heart and the rejuvenation of my blood.

Which left me to wonder... Had the Westside Girl come into my life that autumn in the spirit of Spring, to reinvigorate my marriage with passion—or to exacerbate my yearnings for all that lay outside my promised grasp, thereby pollenating my fields of song?

A single Thursday was all the Westside Girl had promised me, and it was all that I got. After our last swim together, I had the privilege of briefly inhabiting the fantasy I had so often imagined when we met in the parking lot outside the health club. It was the first and only time I ever saw her outside the pool, in her street clothes. She had the furred collar of her coat folded up and was clutching one side of it in a gloved hand that looked dipped in dark chocolate. She wore glasses with delicate bronze frames, their lenses starting to darken in reaction to the bold winter light, perfectly suited to her face and colouring. But what caught me most by surprise was the revelation of her hair.

It was the first time I saw more of her hair than the loose wet tendrils and widow's peak left exposed by her swimming cap. It had the effulgence of Spanish cedar, her hair, a reddish-brown that held a captive golden light within. It was pulled back from her forehead, bowed across her temples and secured in place behind by a system of pins and an antique Victorian comb—zinc alloy I think, something passed down to her perhaps, as it looked of greater sentimental than monetary value. I know this because she did a little spin for me. I was satisfied and not satisfied, because it was hair one could see but also not see, hair whose full treasure of character would become apparent only when the pins and comb were removed, when it was let down, when it was undone in the presence of someone more fortunate than I. No, not more fortunate—fortunate in his own way.

We stood there in our coats, not quite knowing what to say as I shifted my weight from one foot to the other and wanting so much to press my mouth to hers, I asked her to leave me with a memory. She smiled softly and said 'Okay.'

As the softness of her smile turned sly, she flipped me the bird.

I laughed and, as I threw my arms around her, It was impossible to keep secret how my heart was fighting to break out of my chest. When I reluctantly relaxed my arms and stepped back from her, she kept her hand momentarily on my coat, near my waist, and looked briefly into my eyes in a way that hinted she knew more about what had just happened than I knew myself.

The Westside Girl had fulfilled her covenant with me. Nothing was said about a next meeting. It would happen when and if it happened, we tacitly agreed—and, as weeks turned into months, happen it did not. She disappeared back into a life that did not include me, and was replaced in my life by a profound, nameless longing.

Longing, of course, is the romantic form of worry, and I longed for the return of the Westside Girl to my life as much as I also fretted over the possibility. Knowing that she was fond of a certain brand of vodka, I drank that certain brand of vodka—I adopted all of her tastes that were known to me, I supposed, as a way of keeping faith with her. As I kept to my study, I sat and read and smoked and stopped taking calls from friends, not ready nor able to cope with simple, well-meaning questions like "How are you doing?" When I was not writing sad songs, I tore myself on the coral of other questions:

Was it possible, despite all my protestations, that I really loved the Westside Girl?

I tested myself: If I knew she was in trouble, could I help? Would I? Never mind 'would'. *Could* I—with the way I felt about her being my own secret, beyond confession or surrender, without knowing her full name or address?

If not, how could I seriously defend the veracity of my feelings? And if I couldn't, of what use was I to her—even as a friend?

Would I walk away from my marriage to be with her? Did I *have* to? Could I wreck her marriage to be with her? Would I *have* to?

No, no, no.

The Lecturer returns to his keyboard.

None of that was really in the cards, now or ever. What I wanted above all, I realized, was to keep the Westside Girl somewhere in my life, as a source of inspiration, to make her laugh and, yes, to feel loved by her—but why was this so important? Did this lively, jubilantly profane woman matter so much to me because I had passed some impossible milestone in my career and therefore felt that much closer to death?

I couldn't answer any of these questions with finality, and my inability seemed to confirm that she was a fantasy...you'll excuse me for refusing to say '*just* a fantasy...' but shouldn't fantasies, being whatever we want them to be, at the very least be free of pain? Didn't the pain I was feeling challenge my definition of her?

43

All of these questions, I found, could be reduced to one, the most terrifying question of all:

Did I have the courage to live as I dreamed?

I felt the Westside Girl's absence from my life as a form of abject exposure, of nakedness, but her void was a wellspring from which now issued song after song after song, all of them love songs; some of them tender, some of them arrogantly striving for indifference, and one or two of them downright bloody brutal...

With this, the rear curtains swing open once again, revealing the band, as the Lecturer lets rip with his well-loved 'gospel growl' for the first time this evening.

AMBIDEXTROUS HEART

In the middle of the century
I was born at High Noon
Pulled from twixt my mama's legs
In a grey deliv'ry room.

The stars defined me Gemini
Thus I was torn apart
And we would battle, me and I,
For the two halves of my heart.

I've got an ambidextrous heart
Ambidextrous heart
With each beat it sighs
It lives two lives
An ambidextrous heart.

44

I cast no shadow, left or right
I'm the secret no one tells
When I'm sure of where I am at night,
I ache to be somewhere else.

I'm always January
Dressing up for June
I'll be craving sanctuary
From the darkness of my tomb.

I've got an ambidextrous heart
An ambidextrous heart
I've got two Queens in my deck
With their teeth in my neck
An ambidextrous heart

I dwell inside two houses
As I work to pay my dues.
I'm living with two spouses;
One's my Wife and one's my Muse.

Wednesday's child is full of woe
And that's the life I'm livin':
Stuck between the fair of face
And the lovin' and the givin'.

I've got an ambidextrous heart
Ambidextrous heart
But the joke's on me
'Cause if one half breaks
The whole damn thing will fall apart!

Each line is sung at such full throttle, flung arcs of flung saliva are intermittently visible from the front rows. Before the final closing consonant is heard, a trick of the microphone and a trick of the mixing board sustains it, manipulates it, causing it to spin like a helicopter blade or Damocles sword high above the heads of the gathering, transforming the high ceilings of the theater into a citadel of anguish.

The Lecturer momentarily takes it down by lightening his hammering of the keyboard...and then he and the band pick it back up, collectively leaning into the swaggering number, flogging it on to newer and greater heights of delirium. Pounded, whipped, driven to a state of ruin, the music assumes a nearly vertiginous quality, careening gloriously out of control till it rattles to a halt like a dropped plate.

V

T HE LECTURER REMAINS seated at his keyboard, lighting another Consolations to regain his composure.

And then (he continues, exhaling backlit smoke), from a sadly neglected corner of my life, came some sad news—word that my paternal grandfather, Benjamin, had passed away at the age of 94. I had always called him Papa Ben; he had raised me and I loved him as much as any man I've ever known, yet it never occurred to me to write a song for him.

He, however, passed one down to me.

As I mentioned earlier, my father had predeceased his parents on the roadways of America and I grew up with them. Of all the scattered members of my family, my Wife and I were closest to my grandparents, emotionally as well as geographically. My grandmother Marie, well into her eighties, had taught piano in her younger days; she is the only musician in our family other than myself. Without Gran Marie, as I call her, my hands might never have touched piano keys, so my songs might never have been written. She only needed to call and I was on the next flight to Concord.

My Wife was unable to untangle herself from her work obligations that readily, so I flew on ahead to put my arms around my grandmother as she fought to absorb the strongest shock life ever deals to anyone: the sudden and irrevocable loss of half of one's heart.

During my hour-long flight up to Maine, I found myself listening to love songs from the 1920s and '30s, the courtship music of my grandparents' generation. 'Isn't It Romantic?', 'Our Love Is Here To Stay' and 'I've Got You Under My Skin'—these were the songs played on Victrolas at the parties they attended in their youth; these were the melodies that framed their notions of passion as their lips first met, as they danced at their wedding and started a family, as they taught those of their children who could love music to love music.

As I listened to these songs, I found myself thinking about my Wife, who had entrusted her heart to me at the throbbing, even profane, insistence of a very different kind of music. But there was some innate quality to these old songs that prompted sentimental replays in my mind of the scene when we took leave of each other at the airport, when I kissed her face and curled some loose strands of yellow hair behind her ear like I do; but there were other songs in the stream—like 'Where Or When' and 'You Keep Coming Back Like a Song'—that evoked the more haunted, clandestine feelings I associated with the Westside Girl. Those songs brought my restless thoughts back to the closing moments of our only embrace, under that pale winter sky in the parking lot.

Which brings me to another kind of love song, the songs of

courtship. You haven't heard this one before, as it's not one of mine. It's something of a family secret and it's called 'The Smell of Cedar (Makes Me Pine For You)', but I tend to think of it as 'The Woodsy Song'. Listen closely and you'll understand why.

The Lecturer drops his spent cigarette and stares down at his keyboard, striking for a moment the attitude of a tortured artist...but when his spidery fingers finally drop, they bounce! They dance about! Up and down the octaves they cheerfully glide, bringing an unexpectedly lively, endearingly old-fashioned melody into play.

The audience is thrown a curve; even the most ardent of the Lecturer's fans and collectors have never heard this song before, nor have they heard him ever attempt anything like it. For this performance, he adopts a crooner's voice, which seems to emanate from the crackling shellac of an old 78 r.p.m. recording...

THE SMELL OF CEDAR
(MAKES ME PINE FOR YOU)

The smell of cedar makes me pine for you
The most poplar girl in town
I feel I'm from the sticks when close beside you
If you leaf me, I might run aground

I've never said what yew mean to me
But you shiver my timbers where I stand and stood
I'm sycamore things than I care to be
Stay with me—tell me that you wood!

I asked myself when first I sawed you
Are we a-post or in a-cord?

If I sent a note to her out of the blue
Would she write back or would she just be board?
My friends say I've been mulch too shy
They tell me there's a claim that I should stake
'Cause if you splintered off with some other guy
The pain would be im-balsa-ble to take!
Sweet Miss Tree!
The smell of cedar makes me pine for you!

(Ouch!)
I cut myself shavings, deep in thought of you
I tremble like a branch when in your sight
I lumber 'round that I might glimpse you
Wond'ring if your bark's worse than your bite.

I might have to log some overtime
To buy a fir for you—to be exact
'Cause your hazel eyes make me oak deep inside
To give up now would be a birch of contract!

Shall we pull the cork out of a vintage wine
Once we've spruced ourselves up for a date?
Don't be knotty, dearest—try to be on time!
Don't a-banyan me now, don't be late!

Now that you've twigged what you mean to me
I'm countin' on the likelihood
That we'll join hands in ma-tree-mony!
Marry me! Oh, say 'I do!'
Marry me! I'm pitchin' woo!
I doff my cap to you

I'm such a sap for you
Because the smell of cedar makes me pine for you!

The Lecturer gives the number a big, Hollywood finish—so uncharacteristic for such a left-of-the-dial artist. Understanding what he has sacrificed of his insolently cool image to present them with such unbridled corn, the audience responds with their warmest applause of the evening thus far.

Believe it or not (he continues), this epic whack-a-doodle was written—before I was born—by my own Papa Ben. According to the sheet music, he wrote it in 1946, when he was thirty-two years old and already in his twelfth year of marriage. Of course, the 1940s, the war and post-war years, had been a hotbed of wordplay songs, novelty songs, nonsense songs—'Mairzy Doats' and 'Swinging on a Star' spring to mind.

This long-forgotten song was unexpectedly after my Gran Marie asked me, among my other duties as visiting kin, if I might go into Papa Ben's study, a room whose privacy she had always respected and never violated, and separate, as she put it, 'the things I *need* to know about, from the things I *don't* need to know about.' I must confess that I didn't quite understand at first what she meant, but I do now.

It was in a cedar chest at the back of the study closet, appropriately enough, that I found envelopes and folders containing various mementos of my grandfather's romantic youth and what I assumed, from the evidence, to date from his more tormented middle age—photographs of young women he must have known, a few inscribed on the front or back with names like Maeve and Hattie that it's hard to imagine ever carried any kind of romantic or erotic charge. In the same chest I found an envelope containing a lock of hair, still the gleaming

51

russet shade it had been on the day it was cut and presented to him, bound in a simple ribbon. I was awed by the sight of it—it was like a glimpse of my grandmother's faded youth still vibrant as ever in the here-and-now, but I was additionally moved because it could easily have passed for a lock of the Westside Girl's hair.

I raised the bundle to my nose and sniffed it: it was permeated with the scent of the cedar chest where my grandfather hoarded his life's most precious secrets.

It was in a filing cabinet that I discovered the handwritten sheet music for 'The Smell of Cedar.' There were other fragments of musical juvenilia as well, but this song appears to have been Papa Ben's only completed composition. I couldn't quite believe what I was seeing; it revolutionized my idea of the man my grandfather had been. Of all his papers and souvenirs, it stood out for me as his most singular accomplishment.

As my eyes first scanned its music, I must admit that I wrinkled my nose at this bizarre thing I had unearthed. I could intuit, shall we say, a semblance of its fragrance, but it was something I knew myself unable to believe in until I heard it with my own ears. It demanded to be heard, to fill a room with its playful eloquence, so I stopped what I was doing and took the pages to the Baldwin piano in Gran Marie's music room.

The Lecturer turns back to his Yamaha keyboard and reprises a short section of the jaunty melody. He accompanies his own playing, sometimes slowed down for effect, with spoken commentary:

Isn't that lovely? When I first heard this melody take flight, it seemed to throw open the doors of my mind to all the great dancehalls of the past, with their floral wallpaper and chandeliers like the skirts of Christmas trees. It wrapped the lyric in a quaintness I associate with the era in which it was written, a time of big bands and small labels, of songs meant to be played to the steady sway of a cordial bandleader's wand...

He stops playing.

A wretched simulacrum, I've always felt, to be honest, of the true timekeeping of the human heart. Be that as it may, by the time I had played through the second stanza, I had to admit that the words, silly as they were, were also... rather ingenious. Yes, it's quaint; yes, it's old-fashioned; but its expressions of love are unique. Perhaps it's the song's wordplay, its engaging silliness, dare I say its 'fooliage'... (he pauses for laughs and groans)... but *if I had tried with all my heart,* I doubt I could have written a lyric that more perfectly distilled everything my heart had ever wished to express to the women I've wooed in my life. After all, when a man goes a-courting, he does wish to stand out from the pack in the eyes of his chosen one, and what this lyric does is exactly what the male birds do to attract their corresponding kind. When he wrote these words, these wonder-ful puns, Papa Ben was parading his most magnificently coloured plumage, his wit.

The Lecturer resumes playing the melody, this time with increased feeling.

As I played on, I became aware that Gran Marie had walked within my view. She was now watching me play from the French doors separating the music room from the front parlor. I realized, as my hands brought this music back into being, that I felt more in the presence of Papa Ben than I had ever been when we were both flesh and blood—and I could tell from Gran Marie's expression, so startled, so awakened, that she felt the same. My playing was channeling something significant into being, like the proclamation of a truth after decades of repression.

53

As my playing became more familiar with the melody and gained the confidence to add its own filigrees, something clicked—and I tapped into the fullest secret reserves of the song's passion. I could feel the full sweep of its sentimentality, a sentimentality keyed to its moment in history, a sentimentality that becomes so pronounced when it drops into that minor key with (demonstrates on the keyboard) '*You'll never know what yew meant to me ...*'—isn't that lovely? (he stops playing)—and, finally able to see and hear past the puns of the lyric, I found myself genuinely moved... My initial, wryly condescending disbelief of the piece had been wrong—so, so wrong. In its performance I was convinced. This was proud, smart song-writing and, in a manner true to its own epoch and generation, ardent indeed.

As a humble musician herself, Gran Marie had always been supportive of my maverick musical inclinations, even though the music I went on to write and perform was never exactly her cup of tea. This, she told me, was why she came to the threshold of the music room like a ghost when she heard me playing 'The Smell of Cedar'. This was a kind of sentimental music she could appreciate, a music with the power to unlock the doors standing between her and her own lost youth. I assumed that the joy on her face was caused by her reunion with a song she hadn't heard in many, many years—but, rude awakening, she had assumed I was playing for her something new of mine. She had never heard 'The Smell of Cedar' before.

This is how I found out that 'The Smell of Cedar' had *not* been written for my Gran Marie, but had been furtively composed by her beloved husband as an arrow intent upon another heart. It was an accomplishment that Papa Ben had never shared with her.

Think of it: my grandmother had lived with a man for more

than 70 years, had celebrated with him anniversaries that few couples ever attain, without ever knowing that he was a songwriter. To see my poor Gran's face collapse as it glanced for the first time upon a side of her husband's soul that she never knew—that he had never *allowed* her to know, possibly because he felt it would be faithless of him to involve her—seemed an unpardonable cruelty on my part. Even so, she eventually came to share in my excitement over its discovery; after all, it enlarged our memory of this man she loved, and it was a tangible remnant of him, his heart and his mind—but first we had to surmount her breaking down and stammering out that, after a long lifetime together, she hadn't really known her own husband. I tried to impress upon her that this was not her failure, but a failure common to most men.

I thought to console her by producing the envelope where I had found the bound keepsake of her young hair, but quickly shifted gears upon remembering that, throughout their long marriage, Papa Ben had always called Gran Marie his 'dizzy blonde.'

I stayed with Gran Marie for another couple of weeks—not all of it so wrenching or revelatory as the moments I've described, especially after my Wife finally joined us. She held both our hands as we watched my grandfather lowered into the ground in a pre-purchased casket that, I couldn't help noticing, was the proverbial plain cedar box. We could afford better, but it's what he wanted.

As I tackled the mostly mindless work of putting Papa Ben's belongings in some semblance of order and seeing that his few standing bequests were fulfilled, I began ruminating on the deceptive simplicity of romantic love, as it's commonly expressed in love songs, and the many levels where it actually exists for each and every one of us—in reality, where we make our decisions and take action (or don't); in fantasy, where we tease ourselves and explore our options; in our subconscious, where we store the templates and scars left by past loves; and perhaps, as the lock of hair in my grandfather's study proposed, in our DNA as ropes of genetic memory.

What was I to make of this discovery—that my quietly doting and seemingly constant granddad, my centre of gravity while growing up, at some point in his marriage approximate to my own, had felt everything that I was feeling now for a strange woman with the same colour of hair?

Had I been captivated by a genetic template he had passed down to me through the blood we shared?

Was I being solicited by Fate to complete a story that he left unfinished?

And if so, why?

To correct his mistakes, or to ensure their resounding through yet another generation?

VI

THE LECTURER WALKS back into the receptive spotlight haloing his lectern and drinks from his glass once more before advancing to the final act of his performance.

On the flight home, he continues, my Wife and I were exhausted. Once we had settled into our seats, we said little to one another. There now existed the possibility that Gran Marie might come to live with us, which would entail a change of lifestyle that neither of us was eager to confront but had a way of creeping unbidden into every conversation that got started. As my Wife adjusted her earphones to zone out in a space of her own, I listened to bebop at low volume and read *Bullet Park*, in which John Cheever grabbed me by the lapels and asked 'Which came first—Jesus the carpenter or the smell of new wood?'

Jesus, God, religion, communion, crucifixion, the Sacred Heart, stigmata, the resurrection, betrayal—yes, all of these have a special place in the Secret Life of Love Songs. Why do all of these topics, when summoned into music, seem to caress us at the back of our neck, like the lover's cradling hand in the Song of Solomon?

I have heard the argument made that all love songs are addressed to God because God *is* Love. I have often thought to myself that, if there was such a thing as one true God or one true religion, we would all recognize it at once, created as we all are from the same matter. By the same token, I have sometimes asked myself how my Wife could truly be my soul mate when we disagree on so many points, from trivial things like music and movies to the more essential questions, such as what happens to us when we die—materially and spiritually.

My Wife believes in reincarnation, souls reunited after death, that sort of thing. I, on the other hand, am open to whatever happens, while suspecting that all our earthly concerns and relationships become irrelevant at the moment of Death, when we all return like so many droplets into an inconceivably vast ocean of Love that some might call God, our pre-natal memory and craving for which leads us into our various misadventures here on Earth. It is our very inability to imagine the face of God that allows us to find only a diminished and seldom satisfying form of love here on earth, in its billions of scattered facets.

I'm going to let you in on a little secret—a whole bouquet of them, in fact. I had a glimpse of this face on August 11, 2008; it came to me in a dream—one of my life's most remarkable. I remember the date because it was a palindrome of sorts (08-11-08), which seemed a valuable detail at the time, as I scrambled to make sense of it.

In this dream, I was somewhere far away from home and hearth. Go figure. (The audience chuckles.) My Wife, who for some reason figures in my dreams as seldom as she figures in my songs, was as usual nowhere to be found. I was making the rounds in a bizarre high-rise hotel that rose to a leaning angle in the manner of the Tower of Pisa—steep enough for me to feel my own centre of gravity shifting as I explored its baroque interior, admiring its raised ceilings and sunken rooms. I recognized the illuminated, low-lying city outside its panoramic windows as Los Angeles. I was there as the guest of some kind of convention.

The tilting of the structure was so extreme that its elevators had stopped functioning. Nevertheless, I somehow managed to get upstairs to keep an appointment in one of the hotel's penthouse suites, where I was told my guide for the weekend (a talent coordinator with the convention) would be waiting to meet me. The penthouse suite belonged to another guest of the convention, a drama queen who was entertaining a roomful of people with one of his colourful rants.

All I knew about this putative guide assigned to me was that her name was Sophie. I hadn't met her as yet, but I had been advised in advance to memorize her name. As the intolerable host of the penthouse continued to pace and rant and demand everyone's attention like a spoiled child, I played along, knowing that this Sophie must be present here and would introduce herself at the proper moment. And so I waited, biting my tongue and biding my time, wanting very much to get away from there to my own room.

Sophie was indeed there. When the time to leave finally came, she soundlessly conveyed this message to me by standing up as the crowd dispersed and walking to the door backwards. The next thing I knew, we were walking down the corridor together with me suddenly in advance of her, like an object casting her shadow.

I was mysteriously aware that this Sophie was never more than one or two steps behind me, yet I took no real notice of her, nor was I interested in paying her closer attention. Much in the way dreams sometimes allow us to look simultaneously at *and* away from things, I was somehow already aware that she was a skinny, funny-looking girl and not at all my type. I somehow knew that she was short and black-haired, with green eyes and a pale and freckled complexion, dressed in jeans and a butterfly sweatshirt. I found none of this attractive, nor did I care for her name.

Of course I'm friendly to all women, not just those who appeal to me, and my indifference to Sophie was mostly based in maintaining a cordial professional distance, as it seemed to be part of her job description to remain below, or at least outside, my personal radar.

The elevators were at last now functioning. We took a lift downstairs to the hotel's restaurant, which was teeming with the general *hoi polloi* of the convention. As the lift doors parted, Sophie pushed past me; I was on the point of following her inside this teeming mass when by chance I caught sight of an old acquaintance from my waking life, someone whose company I did not care to renew. Not wishing to be seen, I retreated back inside the still-open elevator and went down another floor, opting to skip dinner.

Somehow I found what I knew to be the floor where my room was located, but I had forgotten my room number and had to slip my card-key into the slit of every door until it found one that opened in response.

There is a tittering from somewhere in the balcony seats. The Lecturer is momentarily baffled, having not intended to say anything funny, so he resumes his story.

The opened room was apparently a kind of hospitality suite. No one was there, but as I moved from the doorway to a bar stocked with opened and half-empty bottles . . . to the television

60

set, which still felt warm to the touch…to a table covered in face-up playing cards and poker chips and potato chips, I had the sense that I was being watched. The only thing left to do was lie down, at which point I did not fall asleep so much as wake into another reality, to pass from one dream into another.

I found myself lying supine on a simple mattress dressed with fresh, breeze-dried bedding. The window was open, looking out onto a scene that suggested I was now rooming in a rustic, ground-level California bungalow. This window was the room's only noticeable feature; it looked out upon a courtyard heavily hung with vines and bougainvillea—and suddenly, right there, smiling dreamily at me from the window, was Sophie. Her arms were at rest on the sill, her chin at rest on interlaced fingers. There was someone with her, or at least standing behind her: a gray-haired man who looked harried and impatient, as though both he and she were expected somewhere else. Sophie ignored his worrying, totally absorbed in smiling at me like the proverbial cat sated by the taste of canary.

Sophie's visit felt to me like the most wonderful start a morning could ever have. Smiling, I rose to my feet and crossed the room to the window. I looked down at Sophie from a vantage that showed me that, on the outside of the sill, she was actually sitting astride a bicycle. I was smiling mostly at the situation, amused to find this formerly deflective person now so open and available in her friendliness, and then—seizing a happy, uncomplicated, completely unpremeditated impulse—I bent down and kissed her full on the mouth, more as a friendly greeting than anything else. But her lips clung to mine: she surprised me by returning my kiss generously, with warmth and enthusiasm.

When our kiss ended, some moments later, I felt completely at ease, happy, completely open. I lowered myself to the sill on bended knees, mirroring her position, our foolishly beaming faces perhaps ten inches apart, our gazes locked. It was now that I noticed for the first time the strong definition of the black limbal ring around her irises, which were green and speckled with autumn gold and brown. We smiled at each other that way for some time, utterly shameless, without self-consciousness, somehow ideally paired in this pleasure we were taking in one another. I was only peripherally aware of the worried man standing somewhere behind her, who was now looking rather wilfully down at his own shoes, as though made uncomfortable by the outwardly foolish spectacle we were making of ourselves.

'I was hoping this would have happened last night,' she murmured in her funny voice. It was like receiving a message from the only other person in the world.

What the hell? She had been in the background of my earlier meanderings without receiving any notice from me at all; I had no intimation that she was attracted to me, that she was hoping I would kiss her, or indeed that she had any inner life of her own—as I said, I had barely registered that she existed. But now, a smile and a kiss later, everything outside us had been obliterated. And I do mean literally: the worried man standing behind her a moment ago was now gone, and I knew, the way we know things in dreams, that the bike she had pedaled to my window had likewise vanished, that she was now standing on tiptoe to return the depth of my gaze and it was no effort.

I felt a perfect contentment in her presence. I let my eyes close, and could still feel the nearness of her serene face beating down on mine like summer sunlight. My face was flushed.

I opened my eyes again and she was still there, as I knew she would be, forever and always. Then she broke the silence once more by saying, 'There's really no need for us to wonder if it's ever going to happen again'—and leaned forward to kiss me a second time.

As my eyes closed to meet her, what I felt inside excused every other consideration. Its utter lack of guilt and complication was what made this encounter so wonderful and surprising. As our lips met that second time, I began using my tongue and she responded in kind as if a liquid language were unfolding. I can still feel our kiss as I speak of it now.

At the moment our tongues touched, the sensation was literally electric. Our contact sent bolts of silver energy jolting through me—and I mean *straight through me*, in my mouth and out the other end. The jolts escalated in power in staccato units of three—

Bang! Bang! BANG!

The last of these provoked a mental impression of a radiant silver circle, which I instinctively understood to represent my anus. It was this image that forced me awake, as I pried myself apart from that magnificently celestial, probing kiss—severing my last tie to Sophie—because I was afraid this ardent gift from my dream lover might have literally caused me to shit myself.

Various audience members shift uncomfortably in their seats. The Lecturer lights another Consolations; he has earned it.

Now, says the Lecturer—as a kind of punctuation. It was 'just kissing' of course, but it was also a great deal more. For the duration of those two kisses, for as long as I looked into Sophie's green-and-gold-flecked eyes, I was fully conscious as I occupied the state of my own unconscious, or subconscious—wherever we go when we dream. I awoke next to my Wife with the feeling of having touched tongues in the intimate court of a formidable spirit—a Herald, if not one of the minor Gods, whose gifted saliva had either awakened something long dormant in me or implanted a seed of some sort.

Whatever she was, Whomever she may have represented, I understood in every fiber of my being that Sophie's kiss was not given to just anyone...and I had just been kissed...*and kissed again*.

Then I jumped out of bed to check my underwear.

This addendum elicits more laughter from the audience, mostly from the men in attendance.

When I sing about knowing that someone is out there in 'Under the Nine', I am singing about Sophie—whoever, whatever she may be, *and of whom I had not yet dreamed*—as well as the Westside Girl. It was an extraordinary dream; never before had I known such lucid, tactile consciousness within a dreamscape... *So why did it happen then?*

The only explanation I could muster was that this dream, this visitation, had some wisdom to impart. It had to impress itself on me with sufficient force that I could take its lesson with me back into my waking life. But what lesson could only be conveyed by a kiss so arresting, so involving, so literally electrifying?

This dream did not fade as consciousness took hold, as other dreams do; I came back to bed and lay there for another quarter of an hour, half an hour, three quarters of an hour, incredulous at how the feel and taste and texture of Sophie's kiss lingered on my lips, inside my mouth.

I began analyzing every detail of the dream I could remember. I eventually got up, made a pot of coffee, and reached various conclusions by the time I stepped into the shower.

I could accept the Freudian interpretation: that the tilting hotel represented an erection, that the broken elevator represented fear

64

of sexual dysfunction, which I had in fact experienced with my Wife, off and on, as the weeks since my last contact with the Westside Girl corroded into months and which I attributed to a division in my devotions.

I could also accept the Jungian archetypal view: the pensive old man who vanished from Sophie's side prior to our second, deeper, soul kiss, was Me—the anxious Me, the overthinking Me, the Me that blows things up out of all proportion—in a tense predating of my rejuvenation. The high-rise hotel had stood planted in the flatlands of Los Angeles, the birthplace of my blonde Wife, and the penthouse, with its huffing, puffing host, was an analogy of *The Atlas of What Lives and Breathes*, the zenith of my labors, so obvious in context, as I now look back on it, as to be vulgar.

But who—literally *who on Earth*—was Sophie?

There could be any number of answers to this question. The one I most favor comes from the poet Dante. In his *Vita Nuova*, in which he tells the heartbreaking story of his love for Beatrice and charts its expression in the form of various sonnets written before and after her death, Dante describes two lucid dream encounters with personas that he, upon waking, perceived to be incarnate forms of Love itself. This is whom I finally understood Sophie to be—not the bearded jovial god or the pale and sympathetic young man who appeared to Dante eight hundred years before I was born, but a Valentine sculpted to suit my particular needs.

She was not the complicated, impossible, wrist-slitting Love my old songs had longed for, or in my guilt perhaps felt I deserved, but rather the easy, responsive, curing, nurturing, loving Love I truly needed. Sophie was a brunette but not in the least sullen, a woman I was not prone to worship, but someone

65

whom I could easily take for granted until something in her Cheshire smile drew me irresistibly to her.

I thought again of how the impatient, fretful, aged man looking over Sophie's shoulder had dissolved into thin air as our lips met that second time. It was probing this seemingly minor detail that helped me to see that, over a lifetime, I had deluded myself by thinking that worrying about things somehow brought them more under my control.

My dream's conclusive message, I understood, was that I needed to relinquish my presumption of control, especially in matters of love; it wanted me to know that, if anything as transcendent as my encounter with Sophie was ever going to happen in my waking life, it could only happen spontaneously, by happy and mutual surprise and consent, and could not be coerced into being with the emotional blackmail of promises and covenants and intellectual worry.

It was time to relax my heart's taxing grip and let the Westside Girl go; it was my only prayer of ever recovering the magic I had lost when my thoughts turned to soiled linen.

Then I remembered how Sophie and I had become a team in the penthouse of the drama queen, as my Wife and I had done during the years when my album was being so painstakingly written and recorded. Without her, *The Atlas of What Lives and Breathes* would never have been encouraged or brought to fruition, yet part of me had allied her more with the pain of that mutual struggle than with its eventual triumph. It was something we had survived together, perhaps just barely.

The story of our marriage is very much the story of my Wife and I sharing our dreams with one another. However, as curious as I was to hear her take on this one, I was hesitant to share it. She had gotten out of bed while I was taking my shower. When

I came downstairs afterwards, I saw her through our dining room window, sitting in her robe outside on our patio swing, offering her face to the early morning sun. I poured two cups of coffee and took them outside, where all the colours of an Indian summer day appeared to be heightened, maximized by some force of magic.

I used my elbow to slide the glass door open and stepped onto our back porch, where I felt sunlight touch my arm with a warmth like fondness mailed to me from another place. I looked across the patio to where my Wife was sitting, swinging back and forth, and was astounded to see a large black butterfly, almost the size of a young bat, beating its wings perhaps ten inches away from her face—just hovering there, delighting her with its performance. Not wishing to disturb this minor miracle, I stood silently by the sliding glass door and enjoyed the spectacle.

She turned her eyes to me, wanting to ensure I was there to see this special occurrence but also nervous about looking away from the butterfly for too long, for fear of breaking whatever spell had fallen over the morning. Some moments later, the butterfly flitted away through the air, and I took my place beside my Wife on the swing, the two of us amused and a bit incredulous about this strange communion with nature. We sat there for uncounted minutes, sipping our coffee in silence, seeing our yard enriched by a fleeting Edenic spirit, as birds continued to sing and tiny white butterflies mated here and there in delirious upward spirals.

Somehow, the shared enchantment of that moment made it impossible for me to withhold the details of my dream. With my cup sat down and my head at rest on her shoulder, the story spilled out of me, at first with nervous laughter, then more and more soberly.

The more I told her—about Sophie, about the kiss, about my awareness of the ring on my finger, about how her lips parted, how our tongues touched, even the fear that woke me up—the more I realized that these things, these fantasies, were not outside me; they were part of me. It felt cleansing to entrust them to my Wife; it was one of the entitlements of our relationship.

Later that afternoon, brought closer together by my burst of candour, we spent an unscheduled hour in bed. It has become our habit that my Wife turns her back to me at such moments—I the lover and she the beloved—but this time I was determined to see her face, and I rested my stomach against hers. It was at the height of our entanglement that I looked at her hair, her face and closed eyes (she has a tendency to turn inward during sex), and I said something I had not said to her in many years.

'Look at me,' I said.

As her eyes opened to meet mine, I knew that she was seeing me, really seeing me, in my totality, and I felt positively inseminated with song.

Afterwards, we redressed and went our separate ways to meet the remaining hours of the day. I went into my basement studio and began recording the tracks of a new demo. At the time, I was under the impression that I was working on the first song my Wife had ever inspired, but on further reflection—if I'm being perfectly honest—everything I know about love has been a lesson taught to me by my Wife. Therefore, if the great subject of my work is love, she must, by definition, *abound* in it—be the locus of it, even if she cannot always be the focus of it.

I decided to celebrate the completion of the song by taking a walk with the demo uploaded to my SmartPhone. By then, the sun had started to go down and there was a slight chill in the air, so I wore my jacket. It was while searching my pockets for a cigarette that I found something else in my coat pocket, the pocket where the Westside Girl's hand had lingered after our one and only embrace. It was a card bearing her full name and e-mail address.

They say love is crazy, love is blind, but love often knows us better than we know ourselves. It knows where we must be shepherded, what we must endure, that we may be prepared—prepared for steps that must be taken, in order that the stories or songs we are meant to tell or sing are told and sung.

A decade from now, anything is possible; it is possible that I'll look back on the episodes described in this lecture and have no understanding of how the Westside Girl could have unleashed such volatile emotions, such instability in my life. But the songs that needed to be written passed through a door that might never have existed without her provision.

In ten years' time, having no photograph of the Westside Girl, I might lose the ability to reconstruct her face in memory altogether, perhaps sooner than I think. Were one to exist, in the same time a photo of the Westside Girl might offer me a vision of beauty to which I can no longer relate.

Sad as this is, she will have fulfilled her purpose where I was concerned, by having befriended me when I needed a friend; by having given me an ideal when I needed an ideal; by reminding me of love's heady potency when it reigns fresh and rigorous, and by teaching me a valuable lesson in the importance of not only making love, but keeping it, nurturing it, maintaining it.

By being at the right place at the right time, she gave songs, which would otherwise not have been written, a reason to exist—and those songs, entering into the world, will be heard and perhaps sung by others like so many torches; and in being heard and sung, they will eventually exceed my reach—to touch others, perhaps to help or cure others; just as they helped me to become a better man, a man capable of writing...*this song.*

It's called 'Trust In Love'.

With this, the Lecturer closes his manila folder of crib notes and walks briskly back to his waiting keyboard, whose tone he deftly reconfigures into the acoustic fullness of a concert piano. As he takes his seat on the bench to warm applause, he is rejoined by his bassist, now carrying a bass viol, and his violinist, now equipped with a viola. The three musicians stand about the stage in a triangular arrangement, each of them standing in funneled beams of coloured light—blue for the bassist, amber the viola, and for the Lecturer, wedding white.

TRUST IN LOVE

Trust in love
Trust in love
I may need to grow
But I won't let go
You can trust my love

Trust my love
Dearest love
I can't stay the same
But we share a name
And when push comes to shove
You can trust...my love

As we do the things we must in love
It's important to adjust in love
To change and not to rust in love

70

Forgive those we have cussed in love
When they've mistaken lust for love
And never find disgust in love
When they've fallen in the dust for love
If we can just be just in love
We can trust...in love

Trust in love
Trust in love
It's held us this long
So it must be strong
We can trust in love

Trust my love
Trust my love
I won't let you fall
We can scale this wall
You can trust...my love

As we do the things we must in love
It's important to adjust in love
To change and not to rust in love
Forgive those we have cussed in love
When they've mistaken lust for love
And never find disgust in love
When they've fallen in the dust for love
If we can just be just in love
...we can trust...in love

Trust in love
Little love

I can tell you this
'Cause I have your kiss
...and I trust your love.

Thank you.
Good night.

VII

FTER AN INTERVAL DURING which the house speakers play an alternate recording of "Under the Nine," the Lecturer returns to the stage alone, acknowledging the reception with self-conscious nods of his shaggy head and a brief bow of his storky frame. Seating himself once again at the keyboard, he nervously waits for the silence of the hall to descend once again.

And so it does.

There you have the lecture, he announces, but I must admit—with something not entirely afield of defeat—that it's not quite complete. There is one more piece yet to be performed which, try as I might, I've not been quite able to fit in. It is part of the puzzle yet I find the lecture quite whole enough without it; yet something in me cannot let it stand without being said. Perhaps you'll understand once you hear it yourself. So this is for all you detectives out there, and for those of you more conversant with the strange than I, who know what it is both to have, and have not.

His bony hands dance over the keys in silence until, owing to some programmed delay, the auditorium becomes filled with a strange, cycling music emanating from an old harmonium or hoary accordion. It is prelude to an ode, a confession from the soul to the thirsty dark, a plea and complaint dating from as long ago as the first attempt to make sense of the insensible.

He sings:

FERTILE BARONESS

All lowly regals
Are earthbound eagles
They wade through dry fountains
And glide under mountains

Motionless pounces
On a red square that bounces
When I think I have found it
I just walk around it

Hear now! Songs go unsung
Unfork—my tied tongue
I miss your there-ness
Fertile Baronness

Illegal fairness
My dumb awareness
An unheld opinion of
Abandoned dominion
Toast your demerit
With unrefined claret
Sharpen your focus on

An indistinct locus and

Hear now! Songs go unsung
Unfork—my tied tongue
I miss your there-ness
Fertile Baronness

Replace all your oceans
With unapplied lotions
Dress up, palaver
With indulgent cadavers

Drop anchor and float
As you capsize your boat
Be shamed of your preening
Then abandon all meaning and

Hear now! Songs go unsung
Unfork—my tied tongue
I miss your there-ness
Fertile Baronness

Add my subtraction with
With indistinct action
The loss that's amounted
From numbers uncounted

Celestial hells from
From unsounding bells
Impregnable tatters and
None of it matters so

Hear now! Songs go unsung
Unfork—my tied tongue
I miss your there-ness
Fertile Baronness.

As the Lecturer lifts his hands from the keys, the instrument continues to play while all the time diminishing in volume by iotas. The strokes of the solitary swimmer continue ever on, trailing behind him the primal salts of yearning.

The Lecturer has left the building.

CURTAIN

About the Author

TIM LUCAS is the author of two previous novels, *Throat Sprockets* (1994, included in Jones & Newman's *Horror: Another 100 Best Books*) and *The Book of Renfield: A Gospel of Dracula* (2005), and the Saturn Award-winning critical biography *Mario Bava—All the Colors of the Dark* (2007).

A leading authority on horror and fantastic cinema, he has been editor and co-publisher of the long-running and influential *Video Watchdog* (1990-2017); a critic, columnist and contributor for other magazines from *Sight & Sound* to *Fangoria*; the man behind *Video WatchBlog* for 1500+ entries; and the audio commentator on more than 125 international DVDs and Blu-ray releases.

Now in his 50th year as a professional writer and critic, Lucas has published short stories, reviews, monographs, screenplays, poetry, comics scripts—and now music. He is the proud recipient of 20 Rondo Hatton Classic Horror Awards to date, including (with his wife Donna) the Rondo Legacy Award for Lifetime Achievement.

THE BAND

Singer and composer DOROTHY MOSKOWITZ left an indelible mark on the 1960s as lead vocalist for the highly influential electronic psychedelia band The United States of America. Their only album was first released on Columbia Records in 1968. (It is still available, now with bonus tracks, from Sundazed Records.) Subsequently, she toured and recorded with Country Joe McDonald's All-Star Band, providing backing vocals and piano for his 1973 album, *Paris Sessions*. She later gained notoriety by providing vocals for the spooky cartoon "Cracks," shown in early episodes of *Sesame Street*. In 1997, she won an Izzy (Isadora Duncan) Award for her Japanese fusion score, one of several she composed for San Francisco's Theater of Yugen.

You can hear and learn more about her at her website, www.dorothymoskowitz.com.

GARY LUCAS is widely recognized as one of the world's finest guitarists. Renowned for his past work with Jeff Buckley, Captain Beefheart, The Magic Band, Peter Hammill, and Nona Hendryx, he is also a Grammy Award-nominated songwriter (of Joan Osborne's "Spider Web"). He currently fronts the supergroup Gods and Monsters (which also includes members of Television and The Modern Lovers) and tours the world performing solo recitals and live accompaniment to classic horror and avant grade cinema. He is also the author of *Touched By Grace: My Time with Jeff Buckley*.

MIKE FORNATALE is a singer and multi-instrumentalist based in New York City. Now fronting the all-star collective Murderer's Row, he has performed with several 1960s reunion bands, including The Left Banke, The Monks, and Moby Grape.